A Note to Parents and Caregivers:

Read-it! Readers are for children who are just starting on the amazing road to reading. These beautiful books support both the acquisition of reading skills and the love of books.

The PURPLE LEVEL presents basic topics and objects using high frequency words and simple language patterns.

The RED LEVEL presents familiar topics using common words and repeating sentence patterns.

The BLUE LEVEL presents new ideas using a larger vocabulary and varied sentence structure.

The YELLOW LEVEL presents more challenging ideas, a broad vocabulary, and wide variety in sentence structure.

The GREEN LEVEL presents more complex ideas, an extended vocabulary range, and expanded language structures.

The ORANGE LEVEL presents a wide range of ideas and concepts using challenging vocabulary and complex language structures.

When sharing a book with your child, read in short stretches, pausing often to talk about the pictures. Have your child turn the pages and point to the pictures and familiar words. And be sure to reread favorite stories or parts of stories.

There is no right or wrong way to share books with children. Find time to read with your child, and pass on the legacy of literacy.

Adria F. Klein, Ph.D.
Professor Emeritus
California State University
San Bernardino, California

Editor: Nick Healy
Designer: Abbey Fitzgerald
Page Production: Angela Kilmer
Art Director: Nathan Gassman
Associate Managing Editor: Christianne Jones
The illustrations in this book were created with pastels.

Picture Window Books
5115 Excelsior Boulevard
Suite 232
Minneapolis, MN 55416
877-845-8392
www.picturewindowbooks.com

Printed in the United States of America.

Library of Congress Cataloging-in-Publication Data
Donahue, Jill L. (Jill Lynn), 1967-
The zoo band / by Jill L. Donahue ; illustrated by Aysin D. Eroglu.
p. cm. — (Read-it! readers)
Summary: When this special zoo closes for the day, the zoo animals band comes out
to play.
ISBN-13: 978-1-4048-3165-0 (library binding)
ISBN-10: 1-4048-3165-7 (library binding)
ISBN-13: 978-1-4048-2381-5 (paperback)
ISBN-10: 1-4048-2381-6 (paperback)
[1. Zoo animals—Fiction. 2. Zoos—Fiction. 3. Bands (Music)—Fiction. 4. Stories
in rhyme.] I. Eroglu, Aysin D. (Aysin Delibas), 1968- ill. II. Title.
PZ8.3.D7234Zo 2006
[E]—dc22   2006027298

The Zoo Band

by Jill L. Donahue
illustrated by Aysin D. Eroglu

Special thanks to our advisers for their expertise:

Adria F. Klein, Ph.D.
Professor Emeritus, California State University
San Bernardino, California

Susan Kesselring, M.A.
Literacy Educator
Rosemount–Apple Valley–Eagan (Minnesota) School District

PiCTURE WiNDOW BOOKS
Minneapolis, Minnesota

Something amazing happens when this special zoo closes for the day.

All of the grooving animals come out to play.

Ella Elephant with her trunk blasts a tune.
The pack of furry wolves howls at the moon.

8

The whippoorwill trills a melody that is sweet.
Barney the Bear taps out a happy beat.

11

Lucinda Lion uses a stump for a drum. Two crazy monkeys grab their tails and strum.

Dana Dolphin uses her ringing voice. The others stop to listen. They have no choice.

Oliver Owl joins in with a hooting song.
Ricky Raccoon bangs trash can lids
like a gong.

At last, Randy Rhino makes use of his horn.
Before too long, it's the early morn.

The sun rises, and the zookeeper comes to the gate. The animals know they have played too long and too late.

The animals stop their music when the new day has begun.

They look forward to sunset and more music-making fun!

More *Read-it!* Readers

Bright pictures and fun stories help you practice your reading skills. Look for more books at your level.

Alex and Toolie
Another Pet
The Big Pig
Bliss, Blueberries, and the Butterfly
Camden's Game
Cass the Monkey
Charlie's Tasks
Clever Cat
Flora McQuack
Kyle's Recess
Marconi the Wizard
Peppy, Patch, and the Postman
Peter's Secret
Pets on Vacation
The Princess and the Tower
Theodore the Millipede
The Three Princesses
Tromso the Troll
Willie the Whale

Looking for a specific title or level? A complete list of *Read-it!* Readers is available on our Web site:
www.picturewindowbooks.com